The Pet Sitter

Tiger Taming

Julie Sykes

ILLUSTRATED BY
Nathan Reed

KINGFISHER

For Pat, Cara and Claire

First published 2009 by Kingfisher
an imprint of Macmillan Children's Books
a division of Macmillan Publishers Limited
20 New Wharf Road, London N1 9RR
Basingstoke and Oxford
Associated companies throughout the world
www.panmacmillan.com

ISBN 978-0-7534-1636-5

Text copyright © Julie Sykes 2009
Illustrations copyright © Nathan Reed 2009

The right of Julie Sykes and Nathan Reed to be identified as the
author and illustrator of this work has been asserted by them in
accordance with the Copyright, Designs and Patents Act 1988.

3 5 7 9 8 6 4 2
1TR/1108/MCK/(PICA)/60HLM/C

A CIP catalogue record for this book is available from the British Library.

Printed and Bound in the UK by CPI Mackays, Chatham ME5 8TD

CONTENTS

Chapter One
Wanted

Max ran all the way home from the shops even though it was the hottest day of the summer holidays so far. He arrived out of breath and with a trickle of sweat running down his nose.

'Mum,' he shouted, bursting through the back door, 'can I use the phone?'

'Max!' exclaimed Mum, looking up from the sink where she was peeling carrots. 'What's happened?'

Max stuck a skinny hand into the pocket of his trousers and eased out a scrap of paper. Carefully he laid it on the kitchen table. His heart was thumping loudly; partly because he'd run so fast in the heat and partly because he was scared Mum would say that he couldn't use the phone. He took a deep breath and forced himself to speak slowly and not gabble like he usually did when he was excited.

'Someone needs a pet sitter. There was an advert in the pet-shop window and I wrote it down. Listen to this.'

Max began to read from the slip of paper.

Pet Sitter wanted to look after my cat START NOW GOOD RATES OF PAY Telephone Miss W. Itchy on 08765400223

Mum laughed as she took the scrap of paper from Max and read the advert for herself. Max held his breath and willed her to say yes. He loved animals and was desperate for a pet, but he couldn't have one because of his big sister Alice. Alice was allergic to animals. They made her sneeze and gave her a rash.

'Well,' said Mum thoughtfully, 'it's a good idea, but if you take the job you'll have to see it through to the end. You can't give it up after a few days because you're bored with it.'

'As if!' exclaimed Max. 'I'd never get bored with it. You know how much I want a pet. I'll ring the number then, shall I?'

'Go on then.'

'Thanks, Mum,' said Max, hugging his mother.

Mum wanted to speak to Miss Itchy first so Max punched out her number on the keypad, then handed her the telephone. It rang six times before Miss Itchy answered and when Max heard her voice trill from the receiver his heart skipped a beat. Would the job still be available?

It was! Miss Itchy asked for Max to go round and meet her cat Tiger straight away. Max smoothed his unruly hair with his hands and put on his best, non-holed trainers. He was nervous and keen to make a good impression.

On the way round to Miss Itchy's house, Max tried to remember all the things he knew about cats. They were intelligent and independent creatures and they made good companions. Tiger was a good name, Max decided, imagining a huge stripy cat with tons of energy.

Max walked up and down Sea View Road several times before he found Miss Itchy's home, the Owl House. It was at the end of a narrow alley and Max walked past the entrance three times before he realized it was there! The alley ran between two high brick walls. It was a dark and creepy place and Max glanced nervously over his shoulder, sure that someone was following him. It was a relief when he reached the end of the alley and found a wooden gate with 'The Owl House' painted on it in wonky letters.

Max's hand trembled as he unlatched the gate and made his way along the path. He knew he would make an excellent pet sitter if only Miss Itchy would give him the chance to try. The door had an unusual bell; it was shaped like an owl with eyes that lit up when Max pushed it. It made no sound so Max pushed it again, but harder. This time the eyes flashed amber and from deep inside the house an owl hooted.

'Spooky!' said Max, half wanting to run away.

Suddenly the door opened, revealing a short dumpy lady dressed in black trousers and a gold shirt.

'Max?' she asked, and when Max nodded she smiled toothily and said, 'Come on in.'

Her creaky voice sent a shiver down Max's spine and he didn't move.

'Come along. No need to be shy.'

Miss Itchy wrapped her green fingernails around his arm and before, he could resist, Max was pulled inside the house.

CHAPTER TWO
PLAIN RIDICULOUS

Miss Itchy propelled Max along the hallway and into the kitchen, where black steam erupted from a huge pot boiling on the cooker.

'Ah good, the bat-wing juice is ready,' said Miss Itchy.

She lifted the lid and a bat flew out. Max jumped, but Miss Itchy ignored the bat. Spooning up some of the juice, she blew it cool, then sipped it noisily.

'Delicious! Want a taste?'

Max watched the bat escape through an open window and wished he could fly after it. Suddenly he wasn't sure that he wanted to be Miss Itchy's pet sitter. She was very strange and so was her curious house.

'No thanks,' he said, thinking he'd rather die of thirst than drink that stuff.

'Good-oh! All the more for me,' said Miss Itchy cheerfully. 'Right then. You've come about the pet-sitting job so I suppose you're going to ask me lots of questions.'

Max was surprised. He'd thought that Miss Itchy would want to ask *him* questions. Miss Itchy was the strangest person Max had ever met, but she was smiling in a kindly way so Max asked, 'When are you going away?'

'Right now. As soon as I've put the juice in the fridge. I make it up in bulk once a month.

Tiger loves bat-wing juice, but DON'T feed her any – it makes her do funny things.'

'What shall I feed her?' Max looked around the kitchen, hoping to catch a glimpse of Tiger, but there was no sign of the cat.

'Tiger eats tails. One tin a day, half in the morning and half at night, and a fishy biscuit if she's been good. She has two water bowls, one inside and one out. Everything you need is in the cupboard next to the fridge. Tiger can stay out all day, but bring her in at teatime and lock the cat flap. It's that easy! Any more questions?'

Max had two: why was Miss Itchy going away so quickly and was she, as he suspected, a witch? But the first question

sounded nosey and the second plain
ridiculous, so in the end he just said, 'Can I
see Tiger?'

'Of course you can.'

Miss Itchy opened the back door and
bellowed.

'Tiger,
come here.
You've got a
visitor.'

It was a funny
way to talk to an
animal, but after a bit
a lean black cat with
one green eye and one
blue strolled through
the door. She gave
Max a long, hard
stare before settling

herself in a basket near the cooker to wash her ears. Max stared back, feeling disappointed. This plain, aloof creature was not how he had imagined Tiger to be. Miss Itchy turned to get her purse from a drawer and suddenly Tiger stuck her tongue out at Max.

Max stared. Had he imagined that? Tiger innocently continued her wash, but she was watching Max so he stuck his tongue out in return. Unfortunately Miss Itchy turned and caught him. Max reddened as Miss Itchy gave him a funny look.

'Still want the job?' she asked.

'Oh yes,' said Max. He had a weird feeling that Tiger

was laughing at him, but cats did not snigger or stick their tongues out at people, did they?

'Right then,' said Miss Itchy. 'I'll feed Tiger before I go so you can start tomorrow morning. This is the front-door key and here's your pay and I'll see you in one week.'

Max looked at the notes and coins Miss Itchy had shoved in his hand.

It seemed an awful lot of money for feeding her cat twice a day.

'Tiger's special,' said Miss Itchy, as if she could read his thoughts. 'There'll be BIG TROUBLE if anything happens to her while I'm away. I'm trusting you to take good care of her.'

A shiver tingled down Max's spine. There was no doubt that Miss Itchy meant every word she said. Well, he wouldn't disappoint her. Max would be Miss Itchy's best pet sitter ever. After all, he only had to feed Tiger twice a day. It couldn't be easier!

CHAPTER THREE
THREE BURGLARS

Early next morning Max let himself into the Owl House with the strange feather-shaped key Miss Itchy had given him. An owl hooted loudly when the front door swung open, causing Max to jump. Miss Itchy's house was full of surprises! Max followed the passage along to the kitchen and found it empty. There was no sign of Tiger, and her food from the night before was untouched in her bowl.

'Yikes!' Max exclaimed. It hadn't occurred to him that Tiger might not eat and he wasn't sure what to do next. Should

he throw the food away and give her fresh
food or did Miss Itchy make her eat the old
stuff first?

But when Max looked at the bowl more
closely he recoiled in horror. It was
hardly surprising
that Tiger hadn't
eaten anything.
The dish was full
of tails. Rat tails,
mouse tails and something that might once
have belonged to a cow.

'Gross!'

Max hunted around the kitchen until he
found a spoon, then, letting himself out of
the back door, he scraped the tails straight
into the dustbin. The dish smelt foul and
Max held it at arm's length to wash it clean
in the enormous sink. He took a new tin of

cat food from the cupboard, but when he opened it he found that it too was full of tails!

'Double gross!'

The writing on the tin read: *TAILS. Premium quality cat food. Squirrel and mouse variety.*

'If that's premium quality, I hate to think what economy's like,' said Max.

With his head turned to one side to avoid the smell, Max dished up half the tin and put it on the floor.

But where was Tiger? The cat flap was locked so she had to be in the house somewhere.

'Tiger?'

Max waited, but there was no padding of paws or friendly miaow.

'Tiger, where are you?'

Max listened and suddenly he became aware of voices. His heart beat faster. Who was it? Were there burglars in Miss Itchy's house? Max was suddenly scared. His first thought was to run, but he forced himself to stay calm. He hadn't found Tiger yet, and Miss Itchy had made it clear that there would be Big Trouble if anything happened to her cat while she was away.

Bravely Max crept in the direction of the voices. They were coming from behind a red door on the opposite side of the hall to the

kitchen. Max stood
with his hand on the
doorknob. There was
an argument going
on inside; two girls
were shouting at
each other. They
sounded like fighting
hyenas and reminded
Max of his sister
Alice when she was
in one of her strops.

Max listened, then suddenly he laughed.
He recognized those voices now as belonging
to two characters in a TV soap. Miss Itchy
must have forgotten to turn the television
off before she left. Still laughing, Max
opened the door, then gasped at the sight
before him.

Tiger was sprawled on the sofa surrounded by a pile of fishy biscuits and several empty crisp bags. A can of fizzy lime, sprouting a long bendy straw, was propped up against the cushions beside her. The television was on with the sound at full blast and Max quickly reached for the remote control to turn the volume down.

Tiger twisted her head round and glared at Max.

'Turn it up. I'm watching this.'

'Pardon?'

For a second Max thought that it was Tiger who'd spoken, but, realizing how ridiculous that was, he glanced around to see who else was there. The room was empty.

'Turn it up, birdbrain!'

'No, I won't, dogbreath!' Max retorted, then suddenly realizing he was arguing with a cat he added, 'You can talk?'

'So? Don't tell me you've never heard a cat talk before.'

'No!' said Max excitedly, 'I haven't.'

'Fish-for-brains! Turn the TV up and go away.'

'Fish-for-brains yourself. I'm Max, your pet sitter. Remember me now? I'm looking after you this week.'

'Pet sitter! Ha! That's a joke! I don't need a boy to look after me.'

Max's excitement at finding a talking cat fizzled away like a spent firework. He had always wanted to be able to communicate with animals – just his luck to get a stroppy one!

'Look,' he said firmly, 'Miss Itchy asked me to look after you, and I promised her I would. I've put your breakfast in the kitchen, so off you trot like a good little pussycat and eat it while I clear up this mess.'

Tiger stood up and stretched. In two nimble jumps she went from the back of the sofa to the top of a tall pine dresser, from where she stared defiantly down at Max.

'Make me,' she said.

CHAPTER FOUR

BAT-WING JUICE

Max was furious but he fought back his rising temper.

'Come down,' he said. 'It's dangerous up there.'

'Fish-face!' said Tiger, rudely sticking her tongue out.

Max glanced at his watch. He'd been longer than he thought, and if he didn't go home soon, Mum would worry. It was tempting to leave Tiger where she was, but suppose she fell and hurt herself? Miss Itchy would blame him and Max did not want to get on her wrong side! There was only one thing for it. If Tiger wouldn't come down then he, Max, would have to climb up and get her.

There was a straight-backed chair in the corner of the room. Max thought he might be able to reach Tiger if he stood on it. He moved the chair in front of the dresser, but as he straightened up something hit him on the shoulder.

'Ow!'

Max winced and stared at the book that moments before had been propped on the dresser.

Tiger smirked. 'There's more where that came from.'

So far as Max could see, there were no more books on the dresser, but there were plenty of other items that Tiger could throw at him – all of them breakable.

'I'll come down if there's bat-wing juice for breakfast.'

'No deal,' said Max, remembering Miss Itchy had warned him not to feed Tiger bat-wing juice.

'Why not?' demanded Tiger. 'Oh, don't tell me! Warble Itchy wants the bat-wing juice all for herself. Greedy pig!'

'You're not allowed bat-wing juice. It makes you do funny things.'

'I can do funny things without drinking juice,' said Tiger. 'Watch this.'

Daintily she flicked her tail and knocked a framed photograph of Miss Itchy off the dresser. The photo fell face down and splinters of glass pinged across the wooden floor.

Tiger laughed raucously.
Then, swishing her tail,
she edged closer to
a dainty china
cauldron.

'Wait!' said Max.

Tiger narrowed her eyes, then lined her tail up with the cauldron. 'This cauldron's special. It cost a fortune.'

That did it! Max knew he'd have to get the photograph frame fixed before Miss Itchy returned from her holiday. He couldn't risk having to buy an expensive china cauldron too. Surely a tiny drink of juice couldn't make Tiger any worse than she already was?

'OK,' he said, holding up his hands in defeat. 'Come down and I'll get you some bat-wing juice.'

CHAPTER FIVE
THE PARTY

Tiger drank daintily, then Max let her out into the garden, where she curled up under a bush to snooze in the morning sun. She seemed more friendly now she'd had some bat-wing juice and Max decided that she might be right about Miss Itchy being greedy.

'I'll be back at teatime,' said Max.

'Don't rush,' said Tiger lazily. 'I'd rather be outside than locked indoors. There's more to do out here.'

Max agreed with that. It was the summer holidays and he'd planned to spend the day on the beach with his best friend, Joe. He couldn't wait to tell Joe about Tiger, only he thought he'd leave the talking bit out. Joe would think that was mad. After all, Max could hardly believe it himself! Max was looking forward to seeing Tiger again.

Straight after tea Max hurried along Sea View Road towards the spooky alley that led to the Owl House.

The little tabby cat that lived in one of the houses next to the alley was sitting on the wall and howled loudly as Max passed by. Max felt the hair at the back of his neck stand up! What could have made the cat cry out like that?

Then Max turned into the alley and heard a terrible screeching reply. Immediately he broke into a run. He had a bad feeling about that noise. It sounded like the tabby was talking to another cat. Max hoped Tiger was all right.

By the time Max reached Miss Itchy's gate he was panting and he had a stitch. He stood for a second to get his breath back. Then, as he opened the gate, he was blasted with ice-cold water.

'Yeow! What the . . .' spluttered Max.

'Bullseye!' screamed a familiar voice and there were howls of laughter.

'TIGER!'

Crossly Max pushed his dripping fringe

off his face and wiped the water from his eyes.

'What was that for?'

'Getting our own back.' The tabby appeared from behind Max and stared nastily at him. 'Now you know how it feels when we're having a singsong at night and someone throws a bucket of water at us.'

'Not me!' said Max indignantly. 'I've never done that.'

'Your dad did last week,' said a ginger cat, appearing out of the bushes and standing next to the tabby.
'We were right in the middle of verse two when your dad opened an upstairs window and threw water over us.'

'Oh well, that makes it all right then,' said Max sarcastically. 'Are you happy now?'

No one bothered to answer so Max said crossly, 'It's teatime, Tiger. You'd better say goodbye to your friends now and come inside.'

'No way!' said Tiger. 'We're having a party. It's Red Eye's eightieth.'

Suddenly cats of all shapes and sizes came out of the bushes and squeezed next to each other on the overgrown path. They didn't look too friendly, and Max took a nervous step backwards. A small grey cat with bright red eyes chuckled, then, holding a bottle to his lips, he took a swig of the contents before passing it on to Tiger.

'What's that you're drinking?' asked Max suspiciously.

'Bat-wing juice.' Tiger smacked her lips noisily. 'Red Eye's witch makes it a lot stronger than Warble Itchy does. It's delicious. Want some?'

'No way! And you've had enough too,' said Max. 'Come along, Tiger. It's time to go in.'

There was a horrible noise like rusty hinges creaking in the wind as the cats doubled up with laughter.

'Come along, Tiger,' they mimicked. 'Time to go in and have your tea like a good little pussycat.'

Tiger laughed with them and stayed where she was, one paw firmly grasping the bottle of bat-wing juice.

It was hopeless! Max couldn't leave Tiger out all night but he didn't have a clue how to get her indoors. Miss Itchy had been right. The juice was definitely having a funny effect. Tiger was swaying slightly and she kept shrieking with laughter for no reason. Max decided his best plan was to make a sudden grab for the cat and carry her indoors. He turned his back on her to make her think he was going home, but before he could grab her Max heard the clatter of claws coming along the alley.

'More trouble!' he groaned, and he was right.

Two powerful dogs were rushing towards the Owl House at such speed Max doubted they would stop. Their enormous bodies took up the whole of the alley with no room to spare so they looked like a monstrous,

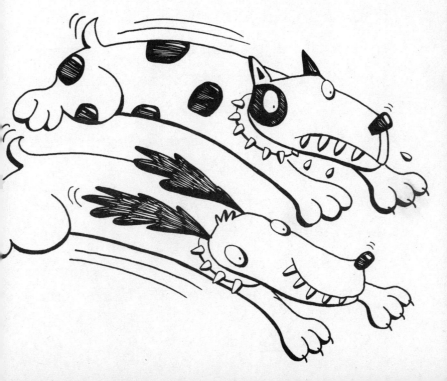

two-headed, eight-legged beast. Max felt
his insides melt.

'Run!' he yelled, and he fled towards the
Owl House.

CHAPTER SIX

THE GATECRASHERS

Max pushed the key into the lock and forced open the front door. Tiger shot in ahead of him and, in spite of his own fear, the sight of her with her fur fuzzed out like a loo brush made Max laugh.

Tiger fled upstairs, and from somewhere in the house an owl let out a blood-curdling screech. Max slammed the front door shut and bolted it for extra safety. Then he ran to the cat flap and locked that too. When he looked out of the window all the cats in Miss Itchy's garden had disappeared. Only the two dogs were visible. Glued

shoulder to shoulder, they prowled slowly around the garden, growling and sniffing at everything.

'Tiger,' called Max, 'where did all your mates go?' There was no reply. Max climbed the stairs and looked around, but Tiger had hidden well and he couldn't find her. Sighing, Max went to the kitchen to dish up her tea. He found the bowl of tails from breakfast untouched. Max didn't dare go outside to put it in the dustbin so he spooned out the rest of the tin on top. He doubted that Tiger would eat it anyway.

Max wondered who the dogs belonged to. He knew most of the local dogs, but he definitely hadn't seen these ones before and they weren't the sort you forgot in a hurry. Max watched out of the window, expecting their owner to come and claim them. But no one appeared and after a long while the dogs left the garden and slunk, side by side, back down the alley. It was getting late, but Max waited another ten minutes to make sure the dogs had gone for good. He didn't fancy meeting them on his way home.

'Bye, Tiger.'

No answer.

'See you in the morning,' Max shouted up the stairs.

As Max let himself out of the Owl House an owl hooted goodbye. Max grinned, thinking the unusual doorbell could teach Tiger a thing or two about manners. At home Max collapsed on his bed. One day over, but six more to go. It seemed an awfully long time to be a pet sitter.

CHAPTER SEVEN
CATNAPPED

The following morning Max vowed he would be firmer with Tiger. He wouldn't let her bully him into feeding her bat-wing juice, and if she started throwing things then he'd threaten to bring the dogs back. Max felt much happier – until he reached the Owl House. He could hear the owl hooting even as he came along the alley. It was going non-stop like a burglar alarm. *Hoo, Hoo, Hoo, Hoo, Hoo!*

With a sinking feeling Max let himself into the house. This had to be something to do with Tiger but whatever was she up to now?

'Tiger!'

Max yelled to make himself heard above the din. 'Tiger, what's going on?'

When there was no answer Max checked the lounge, but this morning the television was off and the room was tidy. The kitchen was empty too and, Max noticed in surprise, so was Tiger's food bowl.

'Poo!' he said, prodding the dish with his toe.

The empty dish reeked and the bowl of water next to it was full of slobber. Max stared at it thoughtfully. Cats didn't slobber, but dogs did and a nasty suspicion crossed Max's mind.

Quickly Max searched the remaining downstairs rooms, then mounted the stairs. The owl doorbell was still hooting and as Max climbed the staircase the

noise grew louder. It sounded
so lifelike that Max wondered
whether he should be looking
for an owl as well as for
Tiger.

'Tiger?' he called.
'Where are you?'

Max searched every
room thoroughly, but
they were all empty.
There was no sign of
Tiger and definitely
no owl. Now Max's
heart began to pound
like running feet.
How could Tiger
have disappeared?
He went back to
the kitchen and

checked the cat flap. It was locked, just as he'd known it would be. Max clearly remembered locking it after the fierce dogs had chased him into the house.

Unsure what to do next Max went back to the hall and collided with Red Eye, who had run in through the open front door.

'Thank goodness you're here,' panted the little grey cat. 'Tiger's in trouble. You've got to save her.'

'Save her from what?' asked Max, wondering if this was another practical joke.

'Grimboots,' said Red Eye.

'Grimboots who?'

'GRIMBOOTS!' shouted Red Eye, and Max saw he was trembling. 'You must have heard of Grimboots. He's the meanest wizard in the world. His dogs took Tiger away last night and they said Grimboots is going to turn her into a pair of gloves.'

CHAPTER EIGHT

HELP ARRIVES

'**A**h, *that* Grimboots!' said Max, deciding this was a joke. 'So how did his dogs get in when all the doors were locked?'

'Magic, of course,' said Red Eye impatiently. 'Can't you hear the sneak alarm going? I'd better turn him off.'

Red Eye leaped up the stairs and opened a small door that Max had thought was a cupboard. The door led into the eaves of the house.

'It's all right, Otus,' called Red Eye. 'Help's arrived. The boy's here.'

Immediately the hooting stopped, and as

Red Eye pulled the door shut Max heard the rustle of wings and caught a glimpse of a large amber eye.

'Oh!' he exclaimed, pleased that the owl was real.

'Go on,' said Red Eye, suddenly brisk. 'Off you go and rescue Tiger.'

'Right,' said Max. 'Silly me! Er . . . so how would I do that then?'

'Go to Seaweed Island and bring her back,' said Red Eye.

'And where is Seaweed Island?'

Red Eye hissed angrily. 'Don't you know Seaweed Island? It's in the middle of the ocean. Grimboots lives there with his dogs.'

'You want me to go to Seaweed Island?' said Max. 'On my own?'

'You're the pet sitter,' said Red Eye. 'I can't go. I hate water and I hate dogs! Besides, this has nothing to do with me. It's Warble's fault. She sold Grimboots a potion to stop his hair from going white, but it didn't work and it made ALL his hair fall out instead. Grimboots is balder than a baby. No hair anywhere, not even up his nose.'

'Couldn't he magic it back again?' asked Max.

'The spell was too powerful,' said Red Eye. 'Warble's gone to see her old teacher to see if she can help to put things right, but Grimboots is so angry he wants revenge. He vowed to get his own back on Warble Itchy and now he has. Tiger is Warble's best friend.'

'And you want me to row over to Seaweed Island and ask Grimboots to give Tiger back?' asked Max incredulously. 'Some chance! His dogs would eat me first!'

'It's too far to row. You'll have to fly,' said Red Eye. 'Luckily Warble left her broom behind. She's too fat to ride it. Off you go then.'

Max's heart began to pound.

'Go now, in the daylight? Won't Grimboots see me coming?'

'Grimboots doesn't go out in the daylight

since he lost his hair. He's gone nocturnal. It's just the dogs you have to worry about. Warble's broom has an invisibility switch so you can fly without being seen. Keep upwind from them so they don't smell you and you'll be fine.'

Max gulped. It sounded simple, but those dogs were vicious. One snap of their enormous jaws and he, Max Barker, would be history. Max was very tempted to run home for his pet-sitting money – he hadn't spent any of it yet. He would give the money back and quit the job. But he remembered what his mum had said and knew it didn't work like that. Once he'd agreed to look after Tiger, the cat was his responsibility until Miss Itchy returned home.

'I can't fly,' he said feebly.

'I'll teach you. It's really easy,' said Red Eye persuasively. 'Warble's broom is in the second room on the right. Go and get it and bring it to the garden.'

The broom was propped against the wall next to a rack of wands. Max sized the wands up, then unhooked the biggest one. It was too long to fit in his pocket but there was a clip on the underside of the broom that made an excellent wand-holder. Max fixed the wand in place, then carried the broom outside.

Chapter Nine
FLYING

'Keep still,' bawled Red Eye. 'You're riding a broomstick, not a bicycle.'

Max stopped pedalling his legs and immediately fell forward.

'Sit up!' Red Eye yelled.

Max tried, but it was really hard to sit straight without feeling like he was going to topple off.

'Sit up!' shouted Red Eye again as the broom lurched into a dive.

Max sat up too quickly. The broom wobbled and he fell off, landing in Miss Itchy's compost heap.

'Yuck!'

Max picked a slug out of his hair and a banana skin from his shoe.

'You've nearly got it,' said Red Eye kindly. 'Let's try again.'

Max had been trying for ages and he didn't feel like he'd nearly got it at all. He was covered in bruises and his bottom hurt

from sitting on the hard broom handle. It was hopeless. He was never going to be good enough to fly to Seaweed Island, let alone rescue Tiger and fly back with her. He might as well face it. He, Max Barker, was in Big Trouble. When Miss Itchy returned and found Tiger was missing, she would probably turn *Max* into a pair of gloves!

But Max didn't give up. Six attempts later he flew a triumphant loop the loop in Miss Itchy's garden. With Red Eye's help he'd done it – he'd finally learned to ride a broomstick! Now all Max had to do was fly to Seaweed Island and rescue Tiger. It sounded easy, but the thought of Grimboots and his dogs made Max feel quite queasy.

'Well done!' said Red Eye, thumping his tail on the ground. 'I'd say you were ready to go.'

'I don't know how to get there,' said Max.

'That's the easy bit,' said Red Eye. 'Tell the broom where you want to go and it'll fly you straight there.'

Max took a deep breath. This was it then. No more excuses. He climbed astride the broom, flicked the invisibility switch on and waved a goodbye to Red Eye. The little grey cat ignored him.

'Bye,' called Max.

Red Eye jumped.

'Don't do that! I thought you'd gone,' he said.

Max chuckled and felt braver now he knew the invisibility switch worked.

'Broom, take me to Seaweed Island,' he commanded.

At first the broom shuddered as if it didn't want to go to Seaweed Island but slowly it rose in the air and flew towards the sea.

It was a sunny day and the beaches were crowded with holidaymakers. Max wondered what would happen if he fell off and became visible again. That would take some explaining!

Seaweed Island was miles away. Max wondered how Grimboots and his two dogs travelled there. Did they fly by broomstick or did they go by boat? Max saw several boats but as he neared Seaweed Island the sea mysteriously emptied.

Remembering what Red Eye had said, Max asked the broom to land upwind of the dogs. The two creatures lived in kennels outside Grimboots's tall stone tower. Max heard them snarling as he flew over the island and prepared to land in a small copse of trees. It was a bumpy landing and Max hoped the dogs hadn't heard him.

He unclipped Warble's wand, then, making the broom visible so he could find it again, he hid the broom under a bush. That was the easy part of the plan and Max was dreading the next bit. Feeling like a burglar, he nervously crept across the island. Even though his feet made no sound, he was sure the noise of his thudding heart would give him away! Several agonizing minutes later Max reached the tower, and there his simple plan to rescue Tiger came unstuck. The

tower had no windows or doors.
So far as Max could see, there was
no way of getting inside!

'Hmmm,' said Max
thoughtfully.

Silently he crept around the
tower, but he found nothing.
There wasn't so much as a crack
in the rough stone walls. There
had to be a way in, but where?
Suddenly the answer came to
Max; if there weren't any doors,
there had to be a secret tunnel.
Max retraced his steps and on
his third time round the tower
he found what he was looking
for – a wooden door almost
hidden in the sandy earth. The
door had no handle and Max

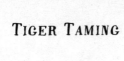

couldn't see a way of opening it until Miss Itchy's wand began to twitch violently.

'Of course!' Max exclaimed, and he pointed the twitching wand at the door.

ZAP!

A jet of gold stars shot from the wand and the door opened.

'Thanks, wand,' whispered Max.

It was dark inside the tower but Max could see two sets of stairs, one spiralling upwards, the other down. He paused, wondering which way to go. He guessed that one of those staircases would lead him to Tiger and the other to the sleeping Grimboots, but which one was which? It was the wand that came to his aid again. It twitched violently, then sent a river of silver stars over the downward staircase.

'Thanks,' whispered Max, and feeling braver because of the wand, he started down the stairs.

CHAPTER TEN
THE RESCUE

Max ran his hand along the rough stone wall as he tiptoed down the staircase. He always got butterflies when he was nervous, but right now his stomach was fluttering like it was full of bats! It was a long way down, but finally Max reached the bottom. A steel door barred his way. Frustrated, Max banged on it, then jumped as something on the other side squealed.

Recovering himself, Max examined the door. There was a small square flap cut into the bottom. Max crouched down and saw the flap was secured with a single bolt.

Wondering what he would find, Max slid the bolt back, then pushed at the flap. It opened inwards and Max held it up with one hand while he peered through it. A cold, damp smell wafted out and Max wrinkled his nose in disgust. His eyes searched the gloom and after a bit he made out a shadowy form huddled in the corner.

'Tiger?' he whispered.

'Max!'

The shadow grew like a balloon, then split apart into three shapes. Cats. Two stayed where they were but the skinny black cat with odd coloured eyes came to the door to stare accusingly at Max.

'What kept you?' hissed Tiger crossly. 'You've been ages.'

'Charming,' said Max. 'I'll go away if you're going to be grumpy.'

'No, wait,' said Tiger. 'I didn't mean it. Please get me out of here.'

Max grinned to himself. It was the first time he'd heard Tiger say please.

The other cats came over and pushed their noses through the flap.

'Will you rescue us too?' they asked.

'Yes,' said Max. 'Stand back. We don't have much time.'

Max was beginning to enjoy the power of Miss Itchy's wand. He waved it around, then rapped it smartly on the door. There was a loud crack and a jet of red flame blasted the hinges skywards. The door groaned then fell inwards, almost squashing Tiger and her cellmates.

'Wicked!' exclaimed Max.

'Careful!' snapped Tiger, picking her way through the wreckage. 'That's Warble's most powerful wand!'

The two other cats ran out of their prison cell and wrapped themselves around Max's legs.

'Thank you for saving us,' miaowed the cat with the white paws. 'I'm Left and this is my brother, Right. Grimboots was going to turn us into earmuffs.'

The more Max heard about Grimboots, the less he wanted to meet him. Quickly he led everyone back up the stairs and out through the trapdoor in the ground. The three cats blinked and sneezed in the sunlight and Max gave them a few seconds to get used to the brightness before moving on.

It was a relief to leave Grimboots's sinister tower behind, and Max gave a silent cheer when they finally reached the copse of trees where he'd hidden the broom.

'We did it!' he whispered triumphantly. 'We're free!'

But Max had spoken too soon. To his horror, when he crawled under the bush to retrieve the hidden broom, he found nothing.

'You probably hid it somewhere else,' said Tiger.

'I didn't!' Max insisted.

Suddenly Tiger went rigid. Her fur stood out like porcupine quills. Then, hissing like a steam train, she launched herself into the nearest tree. Left and Right followed.

Behind him Max heard the scrabble of claws and a fearful snarling.

'Hide!' shrieked Tiger from up in the tree.

Max put one hand on the tree trunk, but before he could climb up, Grimboots's

two thuggish
dogs crashed
into the clearing.

'Lost something?'
snarled one.

The other dog growled and Max gasped, for clamped between the beast's jaws was the missing broom.

At that moment Max's courage failed. Helplessly he watched the snarling dogs come closer.

Move, thought Max. Move now or you'll end up as dog

food. But still his legs wouldn't work. Then he remembered his wand. Max pointed it at the biggest dog.

ZAP!

A jet of orange flame shot towards the dog, who leaped up and swallowed it with one greedy gulp. The dog lunged at Max and snatched the wand from his hand.

Neat trick! thought Max, despite his terror, for what chance did he have now, with no wand to defend himself?

CHAPTER ELEVEN
FIGHTING GRIMBOOTS

'**M**ax!' shouted Tiger.

Max turned and his heart leaped. Tiger was leaning out of the tree with a paw outstretched to help Max to safety.

'Max, quick.'

Max stretched up the tall tree trunk towards Tiger's paw, but he couldn't quite reach it.

'STOP!'

It was a voice not to be argued with and Max froze. A stocky wizard with a billowing cape and tall purple hat strode through the trees.

'So, you're Warble's new apprentice, are you? Not for long!' said the wizard nastily, aiming his wand at Max. 'You'll make a tasty supper for my dogs.'

Max was confused. Who was this? It couldn't be Grimboots, as this wizard had a

fine head of hair. Max could see it sticking out from under his hat in great fuzzy clumps.

Suddenly Max heard something snap. Then a large branch flew out of the tree towards the wizard.

'Run,' shouted Tiger, throwing a second branch.

Max couldn't run. He just stared. Tiger's shot had knocked off the wizard's hat, revealing a bald head shinning in the morning sun. It was Grimboots. The hair was a wig! The wig landed on one of the dog's backs, and the other dog sniffed it suspiciously. In spite of the danger, Max couldn't help himself. He roared with laughter!

'Silence!' shouted Grimboots. 'It's not funny. No one laughs at me.'

Max tried to stop laughing, but he couldn't. It was always like this when he was nervous. Once something started him off, he just couldn't stop; laughing at the wrong thing had got him into trouble heaps of times at school.

'Dogs, get him!'

The dogs ignored Grimboots. They sniffed curiously at the hairy wig, pawing it with their large feet.

Max heard a rustle above his head, then, in a surprise attack, Tiger launched herself at Grimboots. She landed on his back and was joined by Left and Right. Grimboots howled with rage and his dogs flew at the cats. Tiger scrambled on to Grimboots's head and wrapped her paws around his eyes. Grimboots tried to pull her off, but Left grabbed one of his arms

and Right grabbed the
other and together
they pinned them
to his sides.
Grimboots
shook his head
furiously and
Tiger started
slipping.

'Hang on,
Tiger,' yelled
Max.

He was about to join the fight when
he noticed Warble's wand and broom
abandoned on the ground. A better idea
came to him and he seized them both.

'Broom, up,' he commanded, standing
astride it.

The broom rose and Max slid sideways.

He clung on, stopped pedalling his legs, sat up straight and then he was flying properly. The air beneath him was thick with grunts and squawks. Max flew in a circle above the fight while he planned his next move. Then, flicking the broom's invisibility switch on, he whispered, 'Broom, dive.'

The broom obeyed and Max felt he'd left his stomach behind as he sped earthwards. A few centimetres from Grimboots's shiny bald head, Max reached out, grabbed Tiger by the scruff of her neck and zoomed away. Tiger struggled and spat and Max wasted precious seconds convincing her that she was being rescued!

Confident of success, Max dived twice more, snatching first a surprised Left and then Right from Grimboots's arms. The broom dipped with the extra weight and

Max urged it higher. Seconds later Grimboots realized he was fighting his own dogs.

'Fools!' he bellowed angrily.

The dogs caught the scent of the escaping party and jumped and snapped at the empty air. Max flew higher, still skilfully dodging the blue flames shooting from Grimboots's wand.

'HOME!' he commanded and the broom
banked sharply.

Minutes later Seaweed Island was a
shrinking dot in the middle of the sea.

'We did it!' cried Max triumphantly.

CHAPTER TWELVE
MISS ITCHY RETURNS

'You came back then,' said Tiger, as Miss Itchy dumped her suitcase in the hall.

'Hello, Max,' said Miss Itchy.

She ignored her cat and went straight to the kitchen, where she poured herself a large mug of bat-wing juice.

'You came back then,' Tiger repeated, jumping up on the table.

'Juice, Max? No? Good-oh! More for me,' said Miss Itchy, taking a long drink. At last she put the mug down and, wiping her mouth with her sleeve, she asked, 'Why? Did you think I'd gone for good?'

'Didn't know what to think when you scuttled off like that,' said Tiger sulkily. 'You usually take me with you.'

Max was amazed. Suddenly he realized why Tiger had been so awful when he'd first started this pet-sitting job. She hadn't wanted to stay at home.

'Grimboots was after me,' said Miss Itchy. 'Home was the safest place for you.'

'Clearly not,' said Tiger.

Tiger told Miss Itchy what had happened while she'd been away. She was cross with her owner. 'You put Max in a lot of danger,' she said.

'He loved it, didn't you, Max?' Miss Itchy poked Max with a long green nail.

Max grinned and his eyes sparkled as he remembered the adventures of the last week. He'd been more scared than he cared to remember, but Miss Itchy was right. He'd *loved* the excitement and, best of all, he'd made a new friend. Tiger.

'See!' said Miss Itchy triumphantly. 'Max is the *best* pet sitter ever. You'd pet-sit again, wouldn't you, Max?'

'Yes,' said Max, glowing with pride.

'Did you find out how to undo the spell?' Tiger asked grumpily. 'Will Grimboots get his hair back?'

'I know how to fix it, but I've a good mind to

leave him bald after the trouble he's caused,' said Miss Itchy.

'No way!' squawked Tiger. 'Max might not be here for me next time. Give Grimboots the potion.'

Miss Itchy banged her mug on the table.

'All right,' she muttered. 'If I have to. And what about you, Max? Can I give your telephone number to my friends? Pet sitters are hard to find these days, and a good one like you is as rare as Grimboots being nice.'

Max beamed at Miss Itchy. Not only had she called him the best pet sitter ever, but she was offering to get him more pet-sitting work. He could hardly wait to get started!

'Yes, please,' he agreed. 'Max the Pet Sitter is waiting for that call!'

Me and Tiger

ABOUT THE AUTHOR

Julie Sykes has had more than thirty books published including several about her creation, Little Tiger. Among her other titles are *That Pesky Dragon*, *Dora's Eggs* and *Hurry, Santa!*

I Don't Want to Go to Bed! and *I Don't Want to Have a Bath!* won the Nottingham Children's Book Award. Julie has three children and lives in Hampshire.

ABOUT THE ILLUSTRATOR

Nathan Reed has illustrated children's stories for Puffin, HarperCollins and Campbell Books. He also illustrated one of the most popular titles in Kingfisher's *I Am Reading* series, *Hocus Pocus Hound*. Nathan lives in London.